THE PAINTER'S TRICK

PIERO AND MARISA VENTURA

the

PAINTER'S TRICK

RANDOM HOUSE 🏠 NEW YORK

Copyright © 1977 by Piero Ventura. All rights reserved under International and Pan-American Copyright Conventions. Published in the United States by Random House, Inc., New York, and simultaneously in Canada by Random House of Canada, Limited, Toronto.
Library of Congress Cataloging in Publication Data
Ventura, Piero. The painter's trick. SUMMARY: A hungry traveling painter tricks five monks who envision themselves as St. George slaying the dragon. [1. Painters—Fiction] I. Ventura, Marisa, joint author. II. Title. PZ7.V565Pai [E] 76-54411 ISBN 0-394-83320-1 ISBN 0-394-93320-6 lib. bdg.
Manufactured in the United States of America   1 2 3 4 5 6 7 8 9 0

Long ago, in Italy, a painter rode from village to village, painting pictures of saints and madonnas.

One morning he arrived at the gate of a well-kept monastery.

"What luck!" he said. "Surely the monks will want one of my fine paintings. And in exchange I can get some good food . . . and wine."

Ding. Dong. He pulled at the bell.

"Open up, Brothers. A great painter is here!"

Five friendly monks gathered round him in the courtyard, and the painter
showed them a picture of Saint George slaying the dragon. "Wouldn't you like
to have such a work of art on one of your walls?" he asked. "A fine monastery
like this deserves the very best."

The five brothers led the painter to their great hall.

"For many years," said Brother Guardiano, "we have wished for a beautiful fresco to decorate this wall.

"Why don't you paint your picture right here?"

The painter set to work at once, preparing his paints—deep blue for the sky, wine-red for Saint George's cloak, emerald green for the dragon, and many more. As he worked, the smell of cooking floated in from the kitchen.

As soon as the painter had mixed his paints, he started to put up a scaffolding. But soon Brother Guardiano appeared.

"To table! To table!" he called. "Come and share some of our good soup. We make it every day with fresh vegetables from our own garden."

The hungry painter took his first spoonful of the famous soup. What a surprise! It tasted atrocious! He couldn't bear to swallow even one mouthful.

"I don't think I'm very hungry today," he said, and asked to be excused from the table.

"Soup indeed!" thought the painter. "It tastes more like dragon juice. I must think of a way to get something better than that."

While the painter stood thoughtfully in the courtyard, Brother Fornaio passed by with a tray of freshly baked bread for the village. The delicious smell gave the painter an idea.

He walked over to the oven where Brother Fornaio did his baking.

"I was watching you bake, good brother," he said. "And suddenly it came to me that Saint George should have a handsome face—proud and noble—like yours. Will you be my model? It would be a joy to paint a Saint George with your face."

Brother Fornaio was only too happy to pose. While he sat very still on a stool, the quick-witted painter continued to flatter him: "With your shining eyes . . . your perfect nose . . . you will be a great Saint George. And if you could just bake me a small loaf of bread, or a little cake, I think the painting might possibly be even more beautiful."

When Brother Fornaio had finished posing, he baked the most delicious big cake he had ever made. In secret he brought it to the great hall for the painter.

"It will be worth one cake to see myself as Saint George," he thought.

The following day the painter again refused the terrible soup. With his stomach full of cake, he explained, "Every time I paint a Saint George I have no appetite at all."

Once more the painter asked to be excused from the table.

Behind a canvas sheet that hid him from the curious monks, the painter worked on his fresco. But his mind was still on his stomach. "That cake is very good," he thought, "but it will soon be gone. I had better repeat the trick."

When Brother Porcaro came snooping, the painter said, "Ah! Here is my Saint George." And with the same cunning words he had used before, the painter began to flatter Brother Porcaro. The monk blushed . . . and happily agreed to model for Saint George.

After Brother Porcaro had finished posing, he gave the painter an enormous fresh-cured ham. "I was saving it for a special occasion," he said. "But, after all, Saint George is worth a ham like this."

So the days passed. And so Saint George's face kept changing.
The third monk to be a model was Brother Casaro. And the reward?
A rich, creamy cheese!

Next, Brother Ortolano had his turn. He, too, posed in great secret,
thinking ecstatically of a Saint George Ortolano.

This time the reward was a huge basket of luscious ripe fruit.

And, finally, Brother Guardiano posed. Afterwards he gave the painter a jug—no, two jugs—of his precious wine. "It is not often I get a chance to lend my features to a saint as great as Saint George," he said.

At last the painter said the fresco would be ready to show the very next morning. That night the five brothers slept, each dreaming his own dream—of a great saint in a helmet, looking exactly like himself.

As for the clever painter, he was certainly going to be in trouble. His fresco could show only one Saint George, but he had used *five* different models!

Nevertheless, the greedy painter did not seem at all disturbed. He sat in the courtyard beside his mule, feasting on cake and ham and cheese, delicious ripe fruit, and exquisite wine.

Brother Fornaio awoke in the middle of the night. He could not wait to see himself in the finished painting, so he slipped quietly out of bed and crept downstairs. He was going to take a secret peek.

Surprise! Brother Guardiano, Brother Ortolano, Brother Porcaro, and Brother Casaro were already there, looking at him in dismay.

As for the fresco—it was beautiful indeed. A magnificent horse was

charging at a fearful dragon. And on the horse sat a brave Saint George, complete with helmet, cloak, and lance. But his face was the face of the rascal painter!

Never had the five brothers felt such shame.

With downcast eyes, each confessed his vanity. Each told what he had given the painter—a cake, a ham, a cheese, a basket of fruit, and two jugs of the very best wine. But what could they do now?

The following morning the brothers announced they were preparing a great feast to celebrate the finished fresco. The painter was overjoyed, thinking of how he would stuff himself. But he was also worried. What would the five brothers say when they discovered his trick?

The painter soon discovered that the monks could play tricks, too.
When he sat down at the banquet table, his mouth watering . . .

there at his place was a great bowl of the awful soup. Nothing else!
And this time they insisted that he eat it.

That evening the painter rode away on his mule—the taste of the terrible soup still in his mouth. In the future, he decided, he would be a little less greedy. As for the brothers, they still had their wonderful painting. But the face of Saint George would always look down at them—to remind them of their vanity.

PIERO and MARISA VENTURA are a husband-and-wife team who share similar backgrounds. Both were born and raised in Milan, Italy, where they now live with their three sons, and both studied art there at the Brera Academy. Before their marriage, Marisa painted frescoes in Italian churches, an experience which proved valuable when preparing the illustrations for *The Painter's Trick*. Piero trained to be an architect but eventually turned to commercial art and design. He is creative director of one of Milan's leading advertising agencies.

Piero Ventura's Book of Cities, published by Random House in 1975, won an award for excellence in the 1976 Society of Illustrators Annual Exhibition. It was also chosen as one of the Fifty Books of the Year by the American Institute of Graphic Arts (AIGA) and received a Brooklyn Art Books Citation for 1977. An illustration from his second book for Random House, *The Magic Well*, published in 1976, was selected for the 1977 Society of Illustrators Annual Exhibition.